Dedicated with love to our children,
Kailie, Travis, and Gabrielle, and
wonderful childhood memories
of Christmases spent with family
at Stillmeadow Farm in Vermont
and Chapel Hill Farm in Virginia

🐝 little bee books

251 Park Avenue South, New York, NY 10010
Copyright © 2020 by John & Jennifer Churchman
All rights reserved, including the right of reproduction
in whole or in part in any form.
Library of Congress Cataloging-in-Publication Data is available upon request.
Manufactured in China   LEO 0520
First Edition   10 9 8 7 6 5 4 3 2 1
ISBN 978-1-4998-1019-6
littlebeebooks.com

For more information about special discounts on bulk purchases,
please contact Little Bee Books at sales@littlebeebooks.com.

The Christmas Barn

by John & Jennifer Churchman

The sheepdogs watched out the farmhouse window as the rain came down. The autumn storm was fierce.

It tossed the colorful leaves around
and the trees bent low in the wind.
Crack!
In the forest, a tree fell to the ground.

The next morning, after the storm had passed, Farmer John went to look for the fallen tree with Laddie and Maisie. He found the Old Pine Tree lying on the forest floor. It had been the tallest tree on Moonrise Farm for over 150 years.

Now it was gone.

Hmmm . . . he thought. *Maybe the tree can have another life. Maybe we can make a special Christmas gift for the animals.*

That night, Farmer John and his wife, Farmer Jennifer, drew up the plans.

Over the next few days, Farmer John turned the Old Pine Tree into logs. He then rolled the logs into a big pile with his tractor.

He studied the plans for the animals' gift. There was a lot of work to do before Christmas.

Joy the alpaca stopped to watch as he worked. She moved slowly; her belly was big and round.

James the sawyer milled
the logs into boards.
Whir, whir, risp, rasp
went the sawmill.

The chickens, ducks, turkeys,
and geese came running,
curious to see what was going on.

What is this? Cluck, cluck.
What is that? Quack, quack.

Early the next morning, Farmer John
started building the special Christmas
gift for the animals.

First, he cleared a space in the woods
right where the Old Pine Tree had fallen.
Then he marked where the walls would
go with ribbon and stakes.

Mo the farm cat sat
on the old stump
watching curiously.

The sound of Farmer John's hammer rang out through the forest: *thunk, thunk, thunk!*

Finn and Sweet Pea the sheep watched
through the pasture fence as he worked.
They looked at each other and back again.

What can it be?
What can it be?

Farmer John worked every day for many weeks as the weather turned colder and colder.

Brrr, brrrrup went the drill as he made the walls and a roof.
He looked up at the sky. "Winter will be here any day now," he said. "I'll have to hurry."

The alpacas picked their way through the trees to see what Farmer John was doing. Joy put her nose in the air.

Sniff, sniff, snuffle, snuffle. Something smelled different in the forest.

Farmer John was almost finished with the frame. "Snow's coming," he said to himself. He could see his breath in the chilly air.

Meadow the lamb wandered up to see what he was doing. She gave a soft *bahhhh* when she saw him. "Don't worry, little one," he said. "I'm making something to keep you warm all winter."

As he turned back to his work, Farmer John heard the *crunch, crunch, crunch* of leaves. Someone was coming up the path.

It was Farmer Richard with a box full of tools. "Could I lend a hand?" called the old friend.

"Why, yes!" said Farmer John. And together, they made the doors and windows and a beautiful cupola for the roof that afternoon.

All the next day, Farmer John painted. *Splat, swish, splat, swish* went his brush with the dark red paint.

The Highland cows swung their horns this way and that to stay warm, murmuring to each other in gentle *moos* as they watched him work.

It would snow soon, he thought. No time to waste!

The sheep watched as the first snowflakes fell onto their thick woolly coats.

The alpacas huddled around Joy to keep her warm, their feet getting frosty on the snow-covered ground.

That afternoon, as the snow grew deeper, Farmer John spent his time inside building pens and feeders.

He then decorated the gates with balsam garlands and also added something special to the hayloft window.

Early the next morning, Farmer John heard a truck *rumble, rumble, rumble* up the lane. It was his friend Farmer Roger bringing a load of hay to fill the loft.

Sadie the pony looked over the fence. *Hay! Sweet hay!*

The sheepdogs watched thoughtfully from the hillside as the snow started again, falling gently around them.

Farmer John worked all day and into the night, for tomorrow was Christmas Eve!

When the sun rose the next morning over the snow-covered farm, the special gift for the animals was done.
A barn, a barn for Christmas—made from the wood of the Old Pine Tree!

Farmer John and Farmer Jennifer couldn't wait to show the animals their new home. They brought everyone in from the snowy pasture, gave them fresh hay, and took them to their soft beds. Joy the alpaca was the last to come in; Farmer John had made a special place for her right by the window.

That evening, as the animals were settling in, they heard the jingle of bells.

The alpacas and sheep looked up from their hay, and the chickens scurried toward the barn door.

It was their neighbor, Farmer Mariot, with her donkeys. They carried baskets of pumpkins, apples, and corn.

Is that for us?
Is that for us?

"Thank you for the wonderful gifts!" said Farmer John. The donkeys replied with a loud *hee-haw*, but Farmer Mariot just smiled with a twinkle in her eye.

A full moon rose high in the sky that night, rare for Christmas Eve.

Inside the warm barn, Joy gave birth to a little cria.

The animals gathered
around to welcome
the baby alpaca to
the farm.

"I think we'll call her Hope,"
whispered Farmer John.

Farmer John walked outside. It was peaceful and the snow sparkled in the moonlight. He set his hand on the stump of the Old Pine Tree. "You have a new life now. You've become a very fine barn," he said.

"A Christmas Barn for everyone."

He smiled and spoke softly to the animals, safe and snug in their new home.

"Merry Christmas! Merry Christmas to you all!"

Christmas on Moonrise Farm

Christmas on Moonrise Farm is a special time, full of activity. It starts in early winter when we head to the woods to collect evergreen branches to make holiday wreaths and garlands. We collect pinecones and other treasures the forest has to offer to make the decorations special.

All of the animals have a summer home and a winter home on the farm. In the summer, they spend time in the fields eating the green grass and drinking water from the stream to their hearts' content. They take shelter in the cool shade of trees at the edge of the forest. The forest canopy also keeps them dry during summer and fall rainstorms.

In the winter, all the animals are moved to the winter barn (the one we built in this story!) to stay warm, dry, and healthy during the long Vermont winters. Instead of grass from the fields, they have lots of good things to eat from the harvest like hay, corn, apples, beets, and pumpkins. As a special treat at Christmastime, they get to munch on evergreen branches that we have trimmed from the trees in the forest. Farmers John and Jennifer carry buckets of warm water to them all winter long from the farmhouse, sometimes adding herbs and spices to make a warm winter tea.

In 2015, a strong rainstorm hit the farm and flooded many areas of Vermont. The Old Pine Tree that had been on the farm for over 150 years was hit by lightning and fell right on the spot where we turned it into the winter barn. Helped by neighbors, family, and friends, we were able to get the barn ready for the animals to move into their snug new home just in time for Christmas. A Christmas Barn!

About

John Churchman is a photographer, artist, and farmer. Jennifer Churchman is a multimedia artist, storyteller, and writer. John and Jennifer combine their talents to give voice to the stories of the animals that surround them and add boundless enjoyment to their lives. They have made their home on a small farm in the beautiful countryside of Essex, Vermont, with their daughter, Gabrielle.

Special Thanks

This book was created with the support and encouragement of friends, family, and fans of Moonrise Farm. We would like to thank our agent, Brenda Bowen; editor, Charlie Ilgunas; and the whole team at Little Bee Books. We'd also like to give a special thanks to all of the independent booksellers across the country who have championed our books.

The story doesn't end here! Join us for more stories at themoonrisefarm.com.